Earth, Air, Fire & Water

A CHARLOTTE ZOLOTOW BOOK

Earth, Air, Fire & Water

REVISED EDITION

Poems Selected by Frances McCullough

A Charlotte Zolotow Book

Harper & Row, Publishers

Earth, Air, Fire & Water
Copyright © 1971, 1989 by Frances Monson McCullough
Title page art © 1989 by Michael McCurdy
The first edition of this book was published by Coward,
McCann, Geoghegan, New York
All rights reserved. No part of this book may be
used or reproduced in any manner whatsoever without
written permission except in the case of brief quotations
embodied in critical articles and reviews. Printed in
the United States of America. For information address
Harper & Row Junior Books, 10 East 53rd Street,
New York, N.Y. 10022
Typography by Pat Tobin
10 9 8 7 6 5 4 3 2
Revised Edition

Library of Congress Cataloging-in-Publication Data
Earth, air, fire & water.

"A Charlotte Zolotow book."
Summary: This collection of poetry represents the work
of eighty-one contemporary poets including Robert
Creeley, Richard Brautigan, Charles Simic, LeRoi Jones,
Allen Ginsberg, and Sylvia Plath.
1. Poetry—Collections. [1. Poetry—Collections]
I. McCullough, Frances Monson, date.
PN6101.E37   1989   808.81'935   87-45854
ISBN 0-06-024207-8
ISBN 0-06-024208-6 (lib. bdg.)

For David

CONTENTS

INTRODUCTION

This book originally appeared in 1971, long ago enough for its first readers to have offspring nearly ready to read this new edition—or so I imagine. As I look through that book, some of its elements seem dated, particularly its politics and its insistence on rock lyrics being taken seriously as poetry. We're emerging from a much more conservative climate now in 1989, but moving fast toward that nearly unimaginable time: the millennium. If my hypothetical reader searches out a copy of the original book, he may be surprised to see a number of poems missing in this edition. But perhaps the great surprise should be to see so many poems surviving. Authentic poetry seems as fresh and relevant as a letter just opened, and with luck, most of these poems will still have that quality even after the millennium.

Good—and lasting—poetry has always been about the things that are most important to us, and the writing of it has always involved the most delicate and lovely turnings of the mind—in an intellectual and imaginative way, but also in a sensual way, in the exploration of visual patterns and of the splendid possibilities of our language. There are great pleasures in poetry for both the ear and the mouth, and the best way to appreciate them is to read poems aloud, to yourself or to someone else.

The poems in this book were written by all kinds of poets: world famous, unknown, old, under twenty, poets no one ever heard of and poets who aren't usually thought of as poets. They were chosen because of what I see as their excellence, their relevance, their vitality, their wisdom, and most of all what might be called their specific gravity: the pull they exert on their readers.

Discovering poetry is a little like discovering love: You have to be open to it, let it happen to you. If you begin by analyzing it, chances are you may miss it completely. Of course that doesn't mean you'll get everything in it on the first reading (or ever, for that matter) any more than you might expect to understand all the complexities of a person the first time you meet him or her. There's often a strong element of mystery in a good poem that has to be accepted and valued on its own terms. If you've never been excited by a poem, here's an exuberant description of how it feels by Sylvia Plath, one of the strongest poets in this book:

"I recall my mother, a sea-girl herself, reading to me and my brother—who came later—from Matthew Arnold's 'Forsaken Merman.' I saw the gooseflesh on my skin. I did not know what made it. I was not cold. Had a ghost passed over? No, it was the poetry. A spark flew off Arnold and shook me, like a chill. I wanted to cry; I felt very odd. I had fallen into a new way of being happy."*

I hope, of course, that you'll have that kind of reaction to some of the poems that follow. If you do, your enthusiasm should send you elsewhere: to hear poets reading from their work, to bookstores and libraries in search of books by the poets you like most, and—best of all—to your own desk to try writing some poems yourself. If it serves a purpose at all, this book should be just the beginning.

Frances McCullough

*From *The Art of Sylvia Plath,* edited by Charles Newman (Bloomington: Indiana University Press, 1970).

Earth, Air,
Fire & Water

POETRY

I, too, dislike it.
> Reading it, however, with a perfect contempt
> > for it, one discovers in
> it, after all, a place for the genuine.

Marianne Moore

FOR POETS

Stay beautiful
but dont stay down underground too long
Dont turn into a mole
or a worm
or a root
or a stone

Come on out into the sunlight
Breathe in trees
Knock out mountains
Commune with snakes
& be the very hero of birds

Dont forget to poke your head up
& blink
think
Walk all around
Swim upstream

Dont forget to fly

Al Young

THAT FORCE

The force that pulses
in the boughs of trees
and in the sap of plants
also inhabits poems
but it's calm there

The force that hovers
in a kiss and in desire
lies also in poems
though it is hushed

The force that grows
in Napoleon's dreams
and tells him to conquer Russia and snow
is also in poems
but is very still.

Adam Zagajewski
(Translated from the Polish by Renata Gorczynski)

HOW THE SESTINA (YAWN) WORKS

I opened this poem with a yawn
thinking how tired I am of revolution
the way it's presented on television
isn't exactly poetry
You could use some more methedrine
if you ask me personally

People should be treated personally
there's another yawn
here's some more methedrine
Thanks! Now about this revolution
What do you think? What is poetry?
Is it like television?

Now I get up and turn off the television
Whew! It was getting to me personally
I think it is like poetry
Yawn   it's 4 AM yawn   yawn
This new record is one big revolution
if you were listening you'd understand methedrine

isn't the greatest drug no not methedrine
it's no fun for watching television
You want to jump up have a revolution
about something that affects you personally
When you're busy and involved you never yawn
it's more like feeling, like energy, like poetry

I really like to write poetry
it's more fun than grass, acid, THC, methedrine
If I can't write I start to yawn
and it's time to sit back, watch television
see what's happening to me personally:
war, strike, starvation, revolution

This is a sample of my own revolution
taking the easy way out of poetry
I want it to hit you all personally
like a shot of extra-strong methedrine
so you'll become your own television
Become your own yawn!

O giant yawn, violent revolution
silent television, beautiful poetry
most deadly methedrine
                I choose all of you for my poem personally

                          Anne Waldman

SALUTATION

O generation of the thoroughly smug
      and thoroughly uncomfortable,
I have seen fishermen picnicking in the sun,
I have seen them with untidy families,
I have seen their smiles full of teeth
      and heard ungainly laughter.
And I am happier than you are,
And they were happier than I am;
And the fish swim in the lake
      and do not even own clothing.

Ezra Pound

POETS TO COME

Poets to come! orators, singers, musicians to come!
Not to-day is to justify me and answer what I am for,
But you, a new brood, native, athletic, continental,
    greater than before known,
Arouse! for you must justify me.

I myself but wrote one or two indicative words for
    the future,
I but advance a moment only to wheel and hurry back
    in the darkness.

I am a man who, sauntering along without fully
    stopping, turns a casual look upon you and then
    averts his face,
Leaving it to you to prove and define it,
Expecting the main things from you.

Walt Whitman

THE PROPERTIES OF A GOOD GREYHOUND

A greyhound should be headed like a Snake,
And necked like a Drake,
Footed like a Cat,
Tailed like a Rat,
Sidèd like a Team,
Chined like a Beam.

The first year he must learn to feed,
The second year to field him lead,
The third year he is fellow-like,
The fourth year there is none sike,
The fifth year he is good enough,
The sixth year he shall hold the plough,
The seventh year he will avail
Great bitches for to assail,
The eighth year lick ladle,
The ninth year cart saddle,
And when he is comen to that year
Have him to the tanner,
For the best hound that ever bitch had
At nine year he is full bad.

Dame Juliana Berners
(15th century)

WATERMELON

Its got   a good shape/the outside color is green/its one
   of them foods from Africa
its got stripes sometimes like a zebra   or Florida prison
   pants
Its bright red inside/the black eyes are flat and shiney/
   it wont make you fat
Its got heavy liquid weight/the sweet taste is unique/some
   people are shamed of it/
I aint afraid to eat it/indoors or out/its soul food
   thing/Watermelon is what I'm
talking about   Yeah watermelon is what I'm talking about
      Watermelon

Ted Joans

THE APPLE

I am convinced that finally
Isaac Newton ate
The apple that taught him
The law of gravity.

The apple, born of Earth and Sun,
Came into being,
Sprang from the seed,
Ripened
(And before this bees flew to it,
Rain fell and a warm wind blew),
Not so much that it might drop
And by its direct motion demonstrate
That gravity exists,
But to become
                 heavy and sweet,
Beautiful, juicy,
To be admired and picked,
Its scent enjoyed—
And with its sweetness
To delight a Man.

Vladimir Soloukhin
(Translated from the Russian by Daniel Weissbort)

THE LEADEN-EYED

Let not young souls be smothered out before
They do quaint deeds and fully flaunt their pride.
It is the world's one crime its babes grow dull,
Its poor are ox-like, limp and leaden-eyed.

Not that they starve, but starve so dreamlessly,
Not that they sow, but that they seldom reap,
Not that they serve, but have no gods to serve,
Not that they die, but that they die like sheep.

Vachel Lindsay

A LITTLE MORE TRAVELING MUSIC

A country kid in Mississippi I drew water from the well
& watched our sun set itself down behind the thickets,
hurried from galvanized baths to hear music
over the radio—Colored music, rhythmic & electrifying,
more Black in fact than politics & flit guns.

Mama had a knack for snapping juicy fruit gum
& for keeping track of the generations of chilrens
she had raised, reared & no doubt forwarded,
rising thankfully every half past daybreak
to administer duties the poor must look after
if theyre to see their way another day, to eat, to live.

                          *

I lived & upnorth in cities sweltered & froze,
    got jammed up & trafficked
in everybody's sun going down but took up with the
    moon
as I lit about getting it all down up there
    where couldn't nobody knock it out.

Picking up slowly on the gists of melodies, most noises
    softened.
I went on to school & to college too, woke up cold
& went my way finally, classless, reading all poems,
    some books & listening to heartbeats.

Well on my way to committing to memory the ABC
    reality,
I still couldnt forget all that motherly music,
those unwatered songs of my babe-in-the-wood days
until, committed to the power of the human voice,
I turned to poetry & to singing by choice,
reading everyone always & listening, listening for a
    silence deep enough
to make out the sound of my own background music.

Al Young

when i have thought of you somewhat too

when i have thought of you somewhat too
much and am become perfectly and
simply Lustful . . . sense a gradual stir
of beginning muscle, and what it will do
to me before shutting. . . . understand
i love you . . . feel your suddenly body reach
for me with a speed of white speech

(the simple instant to perfect hunger
Yes)
        how beautifully swims
the fooling world in my huge blood,
cracking brains A swiftlyenormous light
—and furiously puzzling through, prismatic, whims,
the chattering self perceives with hysterical fright

a comic tadpole wriggling in delicious mud

E. E. Cummings

YOUNG SOUL

First, feel, then feel, then
read, or read, then feel, then
fall, or stand, where you
already are. Think
of your self, and the other
selves . . . think
of your parents, your mothers,
and sisters, your bentslick
father, then feel, or
fall, on your knees
if nothing else will move you,

      then read
      and look deeply
      into all matters
      come close to you
      city boys—
      country men

      Make some
      muscle
      in your head, but
      use the muscle
      in yr heart

      Leroi Jones

THE RAIN

All night the sound had
come back again,
and again falls
this quiet, persistent rain.

What am I to myself
that must be remembered,
insisted upon
so often? Is it

that never the ease,
even the hardness,
of rain falling
will have for me

something other than this,
something not so insistent—
am I to be locked in this
final uneasiness.

Love, if you love me,
lie next to me.
Be for me, like rain,
the getting out

of the tiredness, the fatuousness, the semi-
lust of intentional indifference.
Be wet
with a decent happiness.

Robert Creeley

BUCKETS

Of rain
hit the buildings
but we in our apartments
are kept dry by the buildings they're in

The rain is rolling off the buildings
and bouncing off
and the roofs keep the rain from getting us wet

the ceiling is not letting any water in

it goes spat spat spat
on the windowledge
trying to get in

the windowpane is streaked with rain
trying to come in

to go everywhere

to make everything wet

I am lying in my bed
head near the window

aware of all this
thinking How Great

We Win

Ron Padgett

RESOLUTION

The ground is white with snow.
It's morning, of New Year's Eve, 1968, & clean
City air is alive with snow, it's quiet
Driving. I am 33. Good Wishes, brothers, everywhere

& Don't You Tread On Me.

Ted Berrigan

I WOULD LIKE MY LOVE TO DIE

I would like my love to die
and the rain to be falling on the graveyard
and on me walking the streets
mourning the first and last to love me

Samuel Beckett

THRUSH

This morning
I heard the sound
Of all my unborn children
Joined into one.

Charles Simic

THIS WORLD

This world drives you out of your mind,
This night, those stars, this fragrance,
This tree bursting with flowers from top to toe.

Orhan Veli Kanik
(Translated from the Turkish by Talat Sait Halman)

FOUR POEMS

It seems a time has arrived
when you've become like those horses
wild with spring
who long for distant fields
where the light mists rise.

*

Though I go to him constantly
on the road of dreams,
never resting my feet,
in the real world
it doesn't equal a single glance.

*

Sent to a man who seemed to have changed his mind

Since my heart placed me
on board your drifting ship,
not one day has passed
that I haven't been drenched
in cold waves.

*

I thought to pick
the flower of forgetting
for myself,
but I found it
already growing in his heart.

Ono no Komachi
*(Translated from the 9th-century Japanese
by Jane Hirshfield and Mariko Aratani)*

Now i lay (with everywhere around)

Now i lay (with everywhere around)
me (the great dim deep sound
of rain; and of always and of nowhere) and

what a gently welcoming darkestness—

now i lay me down (in a most steep
more than music) feeling that sunlight is
(life and day are) only loaned: whereas
night is given (night and death and the rain

are given; and given is how beautifully snow)

now i lay me down to dream of (nothing
i or any somebody or you
can begin to begin to imagine)

something which nobody may keep.
now i lay me down to dream of Spring

E. E. Cummings

WIND AND TREE

In the way that the most of the wind
Happens where there are trees,

Most of the world is centered
About ourselves.

Often where the wind has gathered
The trees together,

One tree will take
Another in her arms and hold.

Their branches that are grinding
Madly together,

It is no real fire.
They are breaking each other.

Often I think I should be like
The single tree, going nowhere,

Since my own arm could not and would not
Break the other. Yet by my broken bones

I tell new weather.

Paul Muldoon

TO KISS A FOREHEAD IS TO ERASE WORRY—

To kiss a forehead is to erase worry—
I kiss your forehead.
To kiss closed eyes is to give sleep—
I kiss your eyes.
To kiss lips is to give water—
I kiss your lips.
To kiss a forehead is to erase memory—
I kiss your forehead.

Marina Tsvetayeva
(Translated from the Russian by John Glad)

TRYING TOO HARD
TO WRITE A POEM SITTING ON THE BEACH

Planted among driftwood
I watch the tide go out
It pulls the sundown with it
& across this scene & against the wind
Man on a motorbike white crash-helmet
His young son rides the gas tank before him
Slows down for the creek mouth
& not too fast up the beach north

Flat dull whistle buoy heard again
And though the wind is right the bell buoy is inaudible

Fat seagull picks at a new hake skeleton
Choosily—not hungry walks away
Returns a moment later,
Room for a few more bites inside

Here comes a family of five
Man prodding with a stick whatever the children test
                with their fingers
Mama is bundled up naturally cold & yellow plastic bucket
Complaining a little ". . . kind of a long way from the car . . ."

The children explore ahead the beach goes on forever & they
Will see it all this evening they aren't tired

Motorbike man coming back slows down for them
        & for the creek mouth
Fog joined into fat clouds cover the sun
Move south stretching rivers & islands of blue
Fine moving sheets & shafts of light on the water horizon

I'm not making it, I'm cold, I go into the house.

Philip Whalen

LILY FLOWER

Lily flower
The telephone is ringing but you do not hear it
Because you are different
You have your own telephone

Michael Brownstein

RECURRING

Fold away your sorrows
In a pretty box.
Fold away your sorrows
Under two quaint locks.
Rats will never find them
To gnaw them through;
Nobody wants them—
They belong to you.
In the lovely darkness
You will find them yet;
You have not forgotten,
You will not forget.
Fold away your sorrows
Safe from moth and mold.
They were never purchased,
They cannot be sold.

Marguerite Young

ANCIENT MUSIC

Winter is icummen in,
Lhude sing Goddamm,
Raineth drop and staineth slop,
And how the wind doth ramm!
     Sing: Goddamm.
Skiddeth bus and sloppeth us,
An ague hath my ham.
Freezeth river, turneth liver,
     Damn you, sing: Goddamm.
Goddamm, Goddamm, 'tis why I am, Goddamm,
     So 'gainst the winter's balm.
Sing goddamm, damm, sing Goddamm,
Sing goddamm, sing goddamm, DAMM.

Ezra Pound

MID-AUGUST AT SOURDOUGH MOUNTAIN LOOKOUT

Down valley a smoke haze
Three days heat, after five days rain
Pitch glows on the fir-cones
Across rocks and meadows
Swarms of new flies.

I cannot remember things I once read
A few friends, but they are in cities.
Drinking cold snow-water from a tin cup
Looking down for miles
Through high still air.

Gary Snyder

SEASON SONG

Here's a song—
stags give tongue
winter snows
summer goes.

High cold blow
sun is low
brief his day
seas give spray.

Fern clumps redden
shapes are hidden
wildgeese raise
wonted cries.

Cold now girds
wings of birds
icy time—
that's my rime.

Anonymous
(Translated from the Irish by Flann O'Brien)

MOVING IN A CARAVAN (1)

I love these old car springs, gulls circling in New Jersey
above dumps, these fire escapes and imaginary cathedrals:
the wrought-iron lamps with dark shores,
and women in Stuyvesant Park carrying bears of snow.
I know the old locomotives lie buried in cemeteries,
and the bones of my father are shining in bank vaults;
I know when I see the dark policeman walking
that we are woven into each other, borne down
in confusion, as in a flood on the Mississippi. . . .

I hear the songs of false love
resonating in the metal all around the stopped clock,
the iron balconies hesitate on Greenwich Avenue,
the opened rabbits, numbly singing in the butcher shops.
I see the fan turning slowly in the metal ceiling,
the shoeform against which the cobbler nails all day. . . .
America is a caravan, we are moving in it,
we will never escape. . . .

Robert Bly

MOVING IN A CARAVAN (8)

We are writing of Niagara, and the Huron squaws,
The chaise-longue, the periwinkles who look like snow,
Dillinger like a dark wind.
Intelligence, cover the advertising men with clear water,
and the factories with merciless space,
so that the strong-haunched woman
by the blazing stove of the sun, the moon,
may come home to me, sitting on the naked wood
in another world, and all the Shell stations
folded in a faint light.

You feel a sadness,
a sadness that rises from the death of the Indians,
from the death of Logan, alone in the house,
and the Cherokees forced to eat the tail of the Great Bear.
We are driven to Florida like Geronimo—
and the young men are still calling to the badger
and the otter, alone on the mountains of South Dakota.

Robert Bly

THE BEACH IN AUGUST

The day the fat woman
In the bright blue bathing suit
Walked into the water and died,
I thought about the human
Condition. Pieces of old fruit
Came in and were left by the tide.

What I thought about the human
Condition was this: old fruit
Comes in and is left, and dries
In the sun. Another fat woman
In a dull green bathing suit
Dives into the water and dies.
The pulmotors glisten. It is noon.

We dry and die in the sun
While the seascape arranges old fruit,
Coming in with the tide, glistening
At noon. A woman, moderately stout,
In a nondescript bathing suit,
Swims to a pier. A tall woman
Steps toward the sea. One thinks about the human
Condition. The tide goes in and goes out.

Weldon Kees

AIR

The sweetpeas, pale diapers
Of pink and powder blue, are flags
Of a water color republic.
The soft bed, turned back,
Is a dish to bathe in them.
This early in the morning
We are small birds, sweetly lying
In it. We have soft eyes,
Too soft to separate the parts
Of flowers from the water, or
The angels from their garments.

Tom Clark

Near the flowering mountain
The immense ocean is seething.
In the comb of my honeybees
There are tiny grains of salt.

Antonio Machado
(Translated from the Spanish by Robert Bly)

THE SNOW

Snow is in the oak.
Behind the thick, whitening
air which the wind drives,
the weight of the sun
presses the snow
on the pane of my window.

I remember snows and my walking
through their first fall in cities,
asleep or drunk
with the snow, desperate falling.
The snow blurs in my eyes
with other snows.

Snow is what must
come down, even if it struggles
to stay in the air with the strength
of the wind. Like an old man,
whatever I touch I turn
to the story of death.

Snow is what fills
the oak, and what covers
the grass and the bare garden.
Snow is what reverses the sidewalk and the lawn
into the substance of whiteness.

So the watcher sleeps himself
back to the baby's eyes.
The tree, the breast, and the floor
are limbs of him, and from
his eyes he extends a skin
which grows over the world.

The baby is what must
have fallen like snow. He resisted,
the way the old man
struggles inside the airy tent
to keep on breathing.
Birth is the fear of death.

Snow is what melts.
I cannot open the door
to the cycles of water.
The sun has withdrawn itself
and the snow keeps falling,
and something will always be falling.

Donald Hall

THE RED WHEELBARROW

so much depends
upon

a red wheel
barrow

glazed with rain
water

beside the white
chickens.

William Carlos Williams

A BLESSING

Just off the highway to Rochester, Minnesota,
Twilight bounds softly forth on the grass.
And the eyes of those two Indian ponies
Darken with kindness.
They have come gladly out of the willows
To welcome my friend and me.
We step over the barbed wire into the pasture
Where they have been grazing all day, alone.
They ripple tensely, then can hardly contain their happiness
That we have come.
They bow shyly as wet swans. They love each other.
There is no loneliness like theirs.
At home once more,
They begin munching the young tufts of spring in the darkness.
I would like to hold the slenderer one in my arms,
For she has walked over to me
And nuzzled my left hand.
She is black and white,
Her mane falls wild on her forehead,
And the light breeze moves me to caress her long ear
That is delicate as the skin over a girl's wrist.
Suddenly I realize
That if I stepped out of my body I would break
Into blossom.

James Wright

IN RESPONSE TO A QUESTION

The earth says have a place, be what that place
requires; hear the sound the birds imply
and see as deep as ridges go behind
each other. (Some people call their scenery flat,
their only pictures framed by what they know:
I think around them rise a riches and a loss
too equal for their chart—but absolutely tall.)

The earth says every summer have a ranch
that's minimum: one tree, one well, a landscape
that proclaims a universe—sermon
of the hills, hallelujah mountain,
highway guided by the way the world is tilted,
reduplication of mirage, flat evening:
a kind of ritual for the wavering.

The earth says where you live wear the kind
of color that your life is (gray shirt for me)
and by listening with the same bowed head that sings
draw all into one song, join
the sparrow on the lawn, and row that easy
way, the rage without met by the wings
within that guide you anywhere the wind blows.

Listening, I think that's what the earth says.

William Stafford

I will bring corn for planting
   and we will make fire
Children will come to your breast
   You will heal my heart
I speak your name many times
The wild cane remembers you

My young brother's house is filled
   I go there to sing
We have not spoken of you
   But our songs are sad
When Moon Woman goes to you
I will follow her white way

Tonight they dance near Chinle
   by the seven elms
There your loom whispered beauty
   They will eat mutton
and drink coffee till morning
You and I will not be there

I saw a crow by Red Rock
   standing on one leg
It was the black of your hair
   The years are heavy
I will ride the swiftest horse
You will hear the drumming hooves

N. Scott Momaday

BEAUTYWAY

Tségihi.
House made of dawn,
House made of evening light,
House made of dark cloud,
House made of male rain,
House made of dark mist,
House made of female rain,
House made of pollen,
House made of grasshoppers,
Dark cloud is at the door.
The trail out of it is dark cloud.
The zigzag lightning stands high upon it.
Male deity!
Your offering I make.
I have prepared a smoke for you.
Restore my feet for me,
Restore my legs for me,
Restore my body for me,
Restore my mind for me,
Restore my voice for me.
This very day take out your spell for me.
Your spell remove for me.
You have taken it away for me;
Far off it has gone.
Happily I recover.
Happily my interior becomes cool.
Happily I go forth.
My interior feeling cool, may I walk.
No longer sore, may I walk.
Impervious to pain, may I walk.
With lively feelings, may I walk.
As it used to be long ago, may I walk.

Happily may I walk.
Happily, with abundant dark clouds, may I walk.
Happily, with abundant showers, may I walk.
Happily, with abundant plants, may I walk.
Happily, on a trail of pollen, may I walk.
Happily may I walk.
Being as it used to be long ago, may I walk.
May it be beautiful before me,
May it be beautiful behind me,
May it be beautiful below me,
May it be beautiful above me,
May it be beautiful all around me.
In beauty it is finished.

Navajo Tribe
(From The Night Chant)

CARRYING MY MIND AROUND

My own mind is very hard to me.
It is just as if I were carrying my mind around.
What is the matter with you?

Tlingit Tribe

DEATH SONG

In the great night my heart will go out.
Toward me the darkness comes rattling.
In the great night my heart will go ou

Papago Tribe

A BIRTH

Inevitably a story with grass,
I find a young horse deep inside it.
I cannot nail wires around him;
My fence posts fail to be solid,

And he is free, strangely, without me.
With his head still browsing the greenness,
He walks slowly out of the pasture
To enter the sun of his story.

My mind freed of its own creature,
I find myself deep in my life
In a room with my child and my mother,
When I feel the sun climbing my shoulder

Change, to include a new horse.

James Dickey

TWO LEGENDS

I

Black was the without eye
Black the within tongue
Black was the heart
Black the liver, black the lungs
Unable to suck in light
Black the blood in its loud tunnel
Black the bowels packed in furnace
Black too the muscles
Striving to pull out into the light
Black the nerves, black the brain
With its tombed visions
Black also the soul, the huge stammer
Of the cry that, swelling, could not
Pronounce its sun.

II

Black is the wet otter's head, lifted.
Black is the rock, plunging in foam.
Black is the gall lying on the bed of the blood.

Black is the earth-globe, one inch under,
An egg of blackness
Where sun and moon alternate their weathers

To hatch a crow, a black rainbow
Bent in emptiness
                    over emptiness

But flying

Ted Hughes

OWLS

—for Camille

Wait; the great horned owls
Calling from the wood's edge; listen.
    There: the dark male, low
And booming, tremoring the whole valley.
    There: the female, resolving, answering
High and clear, restoring silence.
    The chilly woods draw in
Their breath, slow, waiting, and now both
    Sound out together, close to harmony.

    These are the year's worst nights.
Ice glazed on the top boughs,
    Old snow deep on the ground,
Snow in the red-tailed hawks'
    Nests they take for their own.
Nothing crosses the crusted ground.
    No squirrels, no rabbits, the mice gone,
No crow has young yet they can steal.
    These nights the iron air clangs
Like the gates of a cell block, blank
    And black as the inside of your chest.

Now, the great owls take
The air, the male's calls take
  Depth on and resonance, they take
A rough nest, take their mate
  And, opening out long wings, take
Flight, unguided and apart, to caliper
  The blind synapse their voices cross
Over the dead white fields,
  The dead black woods, where they take
Soundings on nothing fast, take
  Soundings on each other, each alone.

W. D. Snodgrass

THE OCTOPUS

Tell me, O Octopus, I begs,
Is those things arms, or is they legs?
I marvel at thee, Octopus;
If I were thou, I'd call me Us.

Ogden Nash

THE ANIMALS

There is a green light which pets feel
that makes them vicious.
They leer from their haven in a bowl
and detest your smell.
Right now, near the sofa,
animals breathe and glow.
The flowers are stiff
in the amber light.
We all need you, tongue, in this room.

Lewis MacAdams

THE FROG

What a wonderful bird the frog are—
When he sit, he stand almost;
When he hop, he fly almost.
He ain't got no sense hardly;
He ain't got no tail hardly either.
When he sit, he sit on what he ain't got—almost.

Anonymous

DANSE RUSSE

If I when my wife is sleeping
and the baby and Kathleen
are sleeping
and the sun is a flame-white disc
in silken mists
above shining trees,—
if I in my north room
dance naked, grotesquely
before my mirror
waving my shirt round my head
and singing softly to myself:
"I am lonely, lonely.
I was born to be lonely,
I am best so!"
If I admire my arms, my face
my shoulders, flanks, buttocks
against the yellow drawn shades,—

Who shall say I am not
the happy genius of my household?

William Carlos Williams

LIFE, FRIENDS, IS BORING

Life, friends, is boring. We must not say so.
After all, the sky flashes, the great sea yearns,
we ourselves flash and yearn,
and moreover my mother told me as a boy
(repeatedly) 'Ever to confess you're bored
means you have no

Inner Resources.' I conclude now I have no
inner resources, because I am heavy bored.
Peoples bore me,
literature bores me, especially great literature,
Henry bores me, with his plights & gripes
as bad as achilles,

who loves people and valiant art, which bores me.
And the tranquil hills, & gin, look like a drag
and somehow a dog
has taken itself & its tail considerably away
into mountains or sea or sky, leaving
behind: me, wag.

John Berryman

POEM

Like musical instruments
Abandoned in a field
The parts of your feelings

Are starting to know a quiet
The pure conversion of your
Life into art seems destined

Never to occur
You don't mind
You feel spiritual and alert

As the air must feel
Turning into sky aloft and blue
You feel like

You'll never feel like touching anything or anyone
Again
And then you do

Tom Clark

ODE TO SOFTNESS

Mornings are blind as newborn cats.
Fingernails grow so trustfully, for a while
they don't know what they're going to touch. Dreams
are soft, and tenderness looms over us
like fog, like the cathedral bell of Cracow
before it cooled.

Adam Zagajewski
(Translated from the Polish by Renata Gorczynski)

TO SATCH

Sometimes I feel like I will never stop
Just go on forever
Till one fine morning
I'm gonna reach up and grab me a handful of stars
Swing out my long, lean leg
And whip three hot strikes burning down the heavens
And look over at God and say
How about that!

Samuel Allen

THE WAKING

I wake to sleep, and take my waking slow.
I feel my fate in what I cannot fear.
I learn by going where I have to go.

We think by feeling. What is there to know?
I hear my being dance from ear to ear.
I wake to sleep, and take my waking slow.

Of those so close beside me, which are you?
God bless the Ground! I shall walk softly there,
And learn by going where I have to go.

Light takes the Tree; but who can tell us how?
The lowly worm climbs up a winding stair;
I wake to sleep, and take my waking slow.

Great Nature has another thing to do
To you and me; so take the lively air,
And, lovely, learn by going where to go.

This shaking keeps me steady. I should know.
What falls away is always. And is near.
I wake to sleep, and take my waking slow.
I learn by going where I have to go.

Theodore Roethke

FURTHER NOTICE

I can't live in this world
And I refuse to kill myself
Or let you kill me

The dill plant lives, the airplane
My alarm clock, this ink
I won't go away

I shall be myself—
Free, a genius, an embarrassment
Like the Indian, the buffalo

Like Yellowstone National Park.

Philip Whalen

THE EYE

The narcissist's eye is blue, fringed with white and
   covered with tempting salad leaves.

The purse-stealer's eye is yellow.

The eye of the non-combatant is white. In the center is
   a target rendered in green and black.

The voluptuary's eye comes to a point. It is like a silo,
   the echo of a halo.

The gravedigger's eye is hollow. It is surrounded by a
   thoroughly contemporary serenity.

The dynamite salesman's eye is like a pool, in which he
   who leans to drink may be lost. Drifting forever, like a
   cloud.

The maiden's eye is tucked under.

The billiard-player's eye comes to a point. It is like a
   mild wine.
      Each billiard-player suffers from imperfect
      nostalgia.

The ghost's eye is green.

The poet's eye is like a candy.

The battleship captain's eye is like the light that falls
   in a glen, when the doe has done with drinking.

The eye of the realist is inflatable.

Michael Benedikt

OUT

Breaking out, trying to find
what my name is, walking the ridge
flat, almost down
                with impatience
rolling words in cigarette papers
the smoke cutting as goodbyes
          the uncertain flames
          gone wet and out.

Waiting for the tracks a tree leaves,
any bed of moss soft enough to love on,
          but not making it.
              Tied into something
              heavy: the sense of myself,
        the flesh I can grab with my hand,
my animal.

Howard McCord

DON'T LET THAT HORSE

Don't let that horse
                    eat that violin

    cried Chagall's mother

                        But he
            kept right on
                        painting

And became famous

And kept on painting
                    The Horse With Violin In Mouth
And when he finally finished it
he jumped up upon the horse
                        and rode away
            waving the violin

And then with a low bow gave it
to the first naked nude he ran across

And there were no strings
                    attached

Lawrence Ferlinghetti

THERE'S A LITTLE AMBIGUITY
OVER THERE AMONG THE BLUEBELLS

ONE: What a poet wants is a lake in the middle of a sentence
(a lake appears)

TWO: yes and a valid pumpkin
(a pumpkin appears)

THREE: and you should slice up language like a meatcutter abba
dabba dabba dabba yack
(sliced up language appears)

FOUR: It's fine we have inhibitions otherwise we'd all be dead
(all drop dead)

FIVE: or flat on our backs
(all roll over onto backs)

SIX: yes and everyone on rollerskates in bed would be nice
(everyone on rollerskates in bed appears)

SEVEN: and a delayed verb

EIGHT: and an old upright piano
(an old upright piano appears)

(all bow together to the audience and to each other)

NINE: goes to the piano and begins to play
(everyone dances)

Ruth Krauss

WARM TEA

Too late, when you show some
unconcern, too late, gentle one person
loving you, honestly, over there
by the space drift, heater
drying her hair. When it's time
she's ready, but
you're due somewhere.
Awash with angels,
reading alone in her chair.

Lewis MacAdams

SONG

The weight of the world
    is love.
Under the burden
    of solitude,
under the burden
    of dissatisfaction

    the weight,
the weight we carry
    is love.

Who can deny?
    In dreams
it touches
    the body,
in thought
    constructs
a miracle,
    in imagination
anguishes
    till born
in human—

looks out of the heart
    burning with purity—
for the burden of life
    is love,

but we carry the weight
    wearily,
and so must rest
in the arms of love
    at last,
must rest in the arms
    of love.

No rest
    without love,
no sleep
    without dreams
of love—
    be mad or chill
obsessed with angels
    or machines,
the final wish
    .   is love
—cannot be bitter,
    cannot deny,
cannot withhold
    if denied:
the weight is too heavy

    —must give
for no return
    as thought
is given
    in solitude
in all the excellence
    of its excess.

The warm bodies
     shine together
in the darkness,
     the hand moves
to the center
     of the flesh,
the skin trembles
     in happiness
and the soul comes
     joyful to the eye—

yes, yes,
     that's what
I wanted,
     I always wanted,
I always wanted,
     to return
to the body
     where I was born.

Allen Ginsberg

O MY LOVE THE PRETTY TOWNS

O my love
The pretty towns
All the blue tents of our nights together
And the lilies and the birds glad in our joy
The road through the forest
Where the surly wolf lived
And the snow at the top of the mountain
And the little
Rain falling on the roofs of the village
O my love my dear lady
The world is not very big
There is only room for our wonder
And the light leaning winds of heaven
Are not more sweet or pure
Than your mouth on my throat
O my love there are larks in our morning
And the finding flame of your hands
And the moss on the bank of the river
And the butterflies
And the whirling-mad
Butterflies!

Kenneth Patchen

BEDTIME

We are a meadow where the bees hum,
mind and body are almost one

as the fire snaps in the stove
and our eyes close,

and mouth to mouth, the covers
pulled over our shoulders,

we drowse as horses drowse afield,
in accord; though the fall cold

surrounds our warm bed, and though
by day we are singular and often lonely.

Denise Levertov

LOSING TRACK

Long after you have swung back
away from me
I think you are still with me:

you come in close to the shore
on the tide
and nudge me awake the way

a boat adrift nudges the pier:
am I a pier
half-in-half-out of the water?

and in the pleasure of that communion
I lose track,
the moon I watch goes down, the

tide swings you away before
I know I'm
alone again long since,

mud sucking at gray and black
timbers of me,
a light growth of green dreams drying.

Denise Levertov

LIVING TENDERLY

My body a rounded stone
with a pattern of smooth seams.
My head a short snake,
retractive, projective.
My legs come out of their sleeves
or shrink within,
and so does my chin.
My eyelids are quick clamps.

My back is my roof.
I am always at home.
I travel where my house walks.
It is a smooth stone.
It floats within the lake,
or rests in the dust.
My flesh lives tenderly
inside its bone.

May Swenson

TAKING HEART

Take me in again, how did I ever doubt
you were right for me, your mouth
beyond reproach, telling me you love me,
lovely, I am, your body is
an ocean, in its own way, saying the same—

so you lose, once more, giving me courage
to go away into the love of others,
lakes & rivers, surely
they'll welcome
a body all of salt.

David Bromige

SPIT 'N IMAGE

pouring honey:
Benjamin

your face folds
out of mine

& mine is a fold
in grandaddy's sweetness
& so on

faces pour
& fold like honey

Coleman Barks

NIMBLE RAYS OF DAY
BRING OXYGEN TO HER BLOOD

After the sponge bath
Spice cake and coffee
In a sky blue china cup

Tiny clouds float by
Like bits of soap
In a bowl of very blue water

A happy baby sleeps
In a silky chamber
Of my wife's lovely body

A leaf spins itself
The leaf's a roof
Over the trembling flower

Everything's safe there
Because nothing that breathes
Air is alone in the world

Tom Clark

MORNING SONG

Love set you going like a fat gold watch.
The midwife slapped your footsoles, and your bald cry
Took its place among the elements.

Our voices echo, magnifying your arrival. New statue.
In a drafty museum, your nakedness
Shadows our safety. We stand round blankly as walls.

I'm no more your mother
Than the cloud that distils a mirror to reflect its own slow
Effacement at the wind's hand.

All night your moth-breath
Flickers among the flat pink roses. I wake to listen:
A far sea moves in my ear.

One cry, and I stumble from bed, cow-heavy and floral
In my Victorian nightgown.
Your mouth opens clean as a cat's. The window square

Whitens and swallows its dull stars. And now you try
Your handful of notes;
The clear vowels rise like balloons.

Sylvia Plath

leroy

I wanted to know my mother when she sat
looking sad across the campus in the late 20's
into the future of the soul, there were black angels
straining above her head, carrying life from our ancestors,
and knowledge, and the strong nigger feeling. She sat
(in that photo in the yearbook I showed Vashti) getting into
new blues, from the old ones, the trips and passions
showered on her by her own. Hypnotizing me, from so far
ago, from that vantage of knowledge passed on to her passed on
to me and all the other black people of our time.
When I die, the consciousness I carry I will to
black people. May they pick me apart and take the
useful parts, the sweet meat of my feelings. And leave
the bitter bullshit rotten white parts
alone.

Leroi Jones

MY CHILD

When I last saw my child
He ate only porridge.
Now he's sad.

He eats bread and meat with a fork and knife
And with manners, which already prepare him
to die politely, and quietly.

He thinks that I'm a sailor,
But knows I have no ship.
And that we have no sea.
Only vast distances, and winds.

My father's movements in prayer
And my own in love
Lie already folded in his small body.

To be grown-up is
To bake the bread of longing,
To sit the whole night long
With a reddening face
Opposite the open oven.

My child sees everything.

And that magic spell, "See you,"
which he's learned to say,
Is only valid among the dead.

Yehuda Amichai
(Translated from the Hebrew by Assia Gutman)

FOR MY DAUGHTER

Looking into my daughter's eyes I read
Beneath the innocence of morning flesh
Concealed, hintings of death she does not heed.
Coldest of winds have blown this hair, and mesh
Of seaweed snarled these miniatures of hands;
The night's slow poison, tolerant and bland,
Has moved her blood. Parched years that I have seen
That may be hers appear: foul, lingering
Death in certain war, the slim legs green.
Or, fed on hate, she relishes the sting
Of others' agony; perhaps the cruel
Bride of a syphilitic or a fool.
These speculations sour in the sun.
I have no daughter. I desire none.

Weldon Kees

GRANDPARENTS

They're altogether otherworldly now,
those adults champing for their ritual Friday spin
to pharmacist and five-and-ten in Brockton.
Back in my throw-away and shaggy span
of adolescence, Grandpa still waves his stick
like a policeman;

Grandmother, like a Mohammedan, still wears her thick
lavender mourning and touring veil;
the Pierce Arrow clears its throat in a horse-stall.
Then the dry road dust rises to whiten
the fatigued elm leaves—
the nineteenth century, tired of children, is gone.
They're all gone into a world of light; the farm's my own.

The farm's my own!
Back there alone,
I keep indoors, and spoil another season.
I hear the rattley little country gramophone
racking its five-foot horn:
"O Summer Time!"
Even at noon here the formidable
Ancien Regime still keeps nature at a distance. Five
green shaded light bulbs spider the billiards-table;
no field is greener than its cloth,
where Grandpa, dipping sugar for us both,
once spilled his demitasse.
His favorite ball, the number three,
still hides the coffee stain.

Never again
to walk there, chalk our cues,
insist on shooting for us both.
Grandpa! Have me, hold me, cherish me!
Tears smut my fingers. There
half my life-lease later,
I hold an *Illustrated London News*—;
disloyal still,
I doodle handlebar
mustaches on the last Russian Czar.

Robert Lowell

ROSEMARY

Pinpoints of green lit up the trees
that early spring day
when a babysitter took her child
for a patient walk through the park.
Be careful, she said, stay close,
don't get lost in this crowd,
don't vanish into smoke.
Rosemary wore blue jeans, a peace sign
pinned to her bag. We didn't know
she was only seventeen, a runaway. In one year
she was to join a cult in California,
four years after that she married
a paralyzed Vietnam Vet.
Eventually they settled together
in the suburban MidWest. Of course,
nobody knew this yet,
that day in the park
among the stone lions and the seals,
the crush and bloom of the idling crowds,
when Rosemary bought her charge a red balloon
and they walked together holding hands
as seriously as lovers.
Soon enough the child fell
and the balloon rose, a red dot
diminishing in the blue sky.

Daniel Pinchbeck

EIGHTEEN

Wet streets. It has rained drops big as silver coins,
gold in the sun.
My mind charges the world like a bull.
Today I am eighteen.

The good rain batters me with crazy thoughts.
Look. Drops are warm and slow
as when I was in a carriage, pinned tight
in diapers, drenched and unchanged for an hour.

Yes, it rained as tomorrow, in the past, always.
The heart scrapes through time, is one heart.
My temples beat stronger than temples of time.

Like a common bum I think of drinking life,
but I am burnt, even by the hot stream of its juices.
I am eighteen.

Maria Banus
(Translated from the Rumanian by
Willis Barnstone and Matei Calinescu)

walking in thought

walking in thought
this land that my fathers seeded
each step a word
which multiplied with history
that man who said
this land was bought
was wrong he was fooling
my grandfathers rested uneasily
they watched their fine songs
playing the games of the gods
until they saw their songs as fools

now i am walking
dreaming singing those foolish songs
who can only cry silent and shamed
my fathers i say and my grand fathers
i see the beauty of your fine songs
and i cannot stop my dreaming.

Simon Ortiz

FATHER'S VOICE

"No need to get home early;
the car can see in the dark."
        He wanted me to be rich
        the only way we could,
        easy with what we had.

And always that was his gift,
given for me ever since,
        easy gift, a wind
        that keeps on blowing for flowers
        or birds wherever I look.

World, I am your slow guest,
one of the common things
        that move in the sun and have
        close, reliable friends
        in the earth, in the air, in the rock.

                    William Stafford

CHRONICLE

I was born the year of the loon
in a great commotion. My mother—
who used to pack $500 cash
in the shoulders of her fur gambling coat,
who had always considered herself
the family's "First Son"—
took one look at me
and lit out
on a vacation to Sumatra.
Her brother purchased my baby clothes;
I've seen them, little clown suits
of silk and color.

Each day
my Chinese grandmother bathed me
with elaboration in an iron tub;
amahs waiting in line
with sterilized water and towels
clucked and smiled
and rushed about the tall stone room
in tiny slippers.

After my grandfather
accustomed himself
to this betrayal by First Son,
he would take me in his arms,
walk with me
by the plum trees, cherries, persimmons;
he showed me the stiff robes
of my ancestors and their drafty hall,
the long beards of his learned old friends,
and his crickets.

Grandfather talked to me, taught me.
At two months, my mother tells me,
I could sniff for flowers,
stab my small hand upwards to moon.
Even today I get proud
when I remember
this all took place in Chinese.

Mei-mei Bersenbrugge

TIES

When I faded back to pass
Late in the game, as one
Who has been away some time
Fades back into memory,
My father, who had been nodding
At home by the radio,
Would wake, asking
My mother, who had not
Been listening, "What's the score?"
And she would answer, "Tied,"
While the pass I threw
Hung high in the brilliant air
Beneath the dark, like a star.

Dabney Stuart

FOR MY FATHER

Being a modest man, you wanted
Expected an ordinary child
And here's this large, inscrutable object

ME

(Buddha's mother only dreamed
of a white elephant;
my mother . . .)

Cross between a TV camera and a rotary press
Busy turning itself into many printed pages
Heavy, a dust-collector, almost impossible
to get off your hands, out of your house
Whatever it was, not an actual child

You recognize part of the works, ones you first donated
But what are they doing—the flywheel horizontal
Spinning two directions at once
A walking-beam connected to a gear train turning camshafts—
Which produces material like this
Sometimes worth money to folks in New York
Or not, nobody knows why.

Philip Whalen

ON THE BEACH AT FONTANA

Wind whines and whines the shingle,
The crazy pierstakes groan;
A senile sea numbers each single
Slimesilvered stone.

From whining wind and colder
Gray sea I wrap him warm
And touch his trembling fineboned shoulder
And boyish arm.

Around us fear, descending
Darkness of fear above
And in my heart how deep unending
Ache of love!

James Joyce

EARTH DWELLER

It was all the clods at once become
precious; it was the barn, and the shed,
and the windmill, my hands, the crack
Arlie made in the axe handle: oh, let me stay
here humbly, forgotten, to rejoice in it all;
let the sun casually rise and set.
If I have not found the right place,
teach me; for, somewhere inside, the clods are
vaulted mansions, lines through the barn sing
for the saints forever, the shed and windmill
rear so glorious the sun shudders like a gong.

Now I know why people worship, carry around
magic emblems, wake up talking dreams
they teach to their children: the world speaks.
The world speaks everything to us.
It is our only friend.

William Stafford

TURNING AWAY FROM LIES

1

If we are truly free, and live in a free country,
When shall I be without this heaviness of mind?
When shall I have peace? Peace this way and peace that way?
I have already looked beneath the street
And there I saw the bitter waters going down,
The ancient worms eating up the sky.

2

Christ did not come to redeem our sins
The Christ Child was not obedient to his parents
The Kingdom of Heaven does not mean the next life
No one in business can be a Christian
The two worlds are both in this world.

3

The saints rejoice out loud upon their beds!
Their song moves through the troubled sea
The way the holy tortoise moves
From dark blue into troubled green,
Or ghost crabs move above the dolomite.
The thieves are crying in the wild asparagus.

Robert Bly

THREE PRESIDENTS

Andrew Jackson

I want to be a white horse!
I want to be a white horse on the green mountains!
A horse that runs over wooden bridges, and sleeps
In abandoned barns. . . .

Theodore Roosevelt

When I was President, I crushed snails with my bare teeth.
I slept in my underwear in the White House.
I ate the Cubans with a straw, and Lenin dreamt of *me* every
    night.
I wore down a forest of willow trees. I ground the snow,
And sold it.
The mountains of Texas shall heal our cornfields,
Overrun by the yellow race.
As for me, I want to be a stone. Yes!
I want to be a stone laid down thousands of years ago,
A stone with almost invisible cracks!
I want to be a stone that holds up the edge of the lake house,
A stone that suddenly gets up and runs around at night,
And lets the marriage bed fall; a stone that leaps into the water,
Carrying the robber down with him.

John F. Kennedy

I want to be a stream of water falling—
Water falling from high in the mountains, water
That dissolves everything,
And is never drunk, falling from ledge to ledge, from glass to glass.
I want the air around me to be invisible, resilient,
Able to flow past rocks.
I will carry the boulders with me to the valley.
Then ascending I will fall through space again:
Glittering in the sun, like the crystal in sideboards,
Goblets of the old life, before it was ruined by the Church.
And when I ascend the third time, I will fall forever,
Missing the earth entirely.

Robert Bly

AT THE BOMB TESTING SITE

At noon in the desert a panting lizard
waited for history, its elbows tense,
watching the curve of a particular road
as if something might happen.

It was looking at something farther off
than people could see, an important scene
acted in stone for little selves
at the flute end of consequences.

There was just a continent without much on it
under a sky that never cared less.
Ready for a change, the elbows waited.
The hands gripped hard on the desert.

William Stafford

A LETTER TO THE YOUNG MEN

When the days grow teeth at last and games
Are over; when sunset stills our eyes and search
Is done, the ways all blocked, the wind's
Majestic house gone slack to the crush
Of quarreling planes in all their blue skies;
When bayonets are dearer than sunflowers
In all the stalls of earth; when your country
Needs you asking Why do naked good bodies
Go up like stale rockets O proud bloody flowers
Growing in History's garden Break it
Up young men   their guns are pointed
At you are pointed at all the mad flaming
Grandeur which killers can never make die.

Kenneth Patchen

ON A HIGHWAY EAST OF SELMA, ALABAMA; JULY 1965

As the sheriff remarked: I had no business being there. He was right, but for the wrong reasons. Among that odd crew of volunteers from the North, I was by far the most inept and least effective. I couldn't have inspired or assisted a woodchuck to vote. In fact, when the sheriff's buddies nabbed me on the highway east of Selma, I'd just been released from ten days in jail in Mississippi. I was fed up and terrified; I was actually fleeing North and glad to go.

*

In Jackson, they'd been ready for the demonstration. After the peaceful arrests, after the news cameras recorded us being quietly ushered onto trucks, the doors were closed and we headed for the county fairgrounds. Once we passed the gates, it was a different story: the truck doors opened on a crowd of state troopers waiting to greet us with their nightsticks out. Smiles beneath mirrored sunglasses and blue riot helmets; smiles above badges taped so numbers didn't show.

For the next twenty minutes, they clubbed us, and it kept up at intervals, more or less random, all that afternoon and into the evening. Next morning we woke to new guards who did not need to conceal their names or faces. A little later, the FBI arrived to ask if anyone had any specific complaints about how they'd been treated and by whom. But late that first night, as we sat bolt upright in rows on the concrete floor of the cattle barn waiting for mattresses to arrive, one last precise event: a guard stopped in front of the ten-year-old black kid next to me. He pulled a "FREEDOM NOW" pin from the kid's shirt, made him put it in his mouth, then ordered him to swallow.

*

That stakeout at dusk on Route 80 east of Selma was intended for someone else, some imaginary organizer rumored to be headed toward their dismal, Godforsaken town. Why did they stop me? The New York plates, perhaps, and that little bit of stupidity: the straw hat I wore, a souvenir of Mississippi. Siren-wail from an unmarked car behind me—why should I think they were cops? I hesitated, then pulled to the shoulder. The two who jumped out waved pistols, but wore no uniforms or badges. By then, my doors were locked, my windows rolled. Absurd sound of a pistol barrel rapping the glass three inches from my face: "Get out, you son of a bitch, or we'll blow your head off." When they found pamphlets on the back seat they were sure they'd got the right guy. The fat one started poking my stomach with his gun, saying, "Boy, we're gonna dump you in the swamp."

*

It was a long ride through the dark, a ride full of believable threats, before they arrived at the hamlet with its cinderblock jail. He was very glad to see it, that adolescent I was twenty years ago. For eight years he cowered in his solitary cell, stinking of dirt and fear. He's cowering there still, waiting for me to come back and release him by turning his terror into art. But consciously or not, he made his choice and he's caught in history.

And if I reach back now, it's only to hug him and tell him to be brave, to remember that black kid who sat beside him in the Mississippi darkness. And to remember that silence shared by guards and prisoners alike as they watched in disbelief the darkness deepening around the small shape in his mouth, the taste of metal, the feel of the pin against his tongue. It's too dark for it to matter what's printed on the pin; it's too dark for anything but the brute fact that someone wants him to choke to death on its hard shape. And still he refuses to swallow.

Gregory Orr

GUNNER

Did they send me away from my cat and my wife
To a doctor who poked me and counted my teeth,
To a line on a plain, to a stove in a tent?
Did I nod in the flies of the schools?

And the fighters rolled into the traces like rabbits,
The blood froze over my splints like a scab—
Did I snore, all still and grey in the turret,
Till the palms rose out of the sea with my death?

And the world ends here, in the sand of a grave,
All my wars over? . . . It was easy as that!
Has my wife a pension of so many mice?
Did the medals go home to my cat?

Randall Jarrell

MY FATHER'S SONG

Wanting to say things,
I miss my father tonight.
His voice, the slight catch,
the depth from his thin chest,
the tremble of emotion
in something he has just said
to his son, his song:

We planted corn one Spring at Acu—
we planted several times
but this one particular time
I remember the soft damp sand
in my hand.

My father had stopped at one point
to show me an overturned furrow;
the plowshare had unearthed
the burrow nest of a mouse
in the soft moist sand.

Very gently, he scooped tiny pink animals
into the palm of his hand
and told me to touch them.
We took them to the edge
of the field and put them in the shade
of a sand moist clod.

I remember the very softness
of cool and warm sand and tiny alive mice
and my father saying things.

Simon Ortiz

THE FINAL TOAST

And now the final toast:
To Mr. Bread who made all this possible
To Mr. Paper who helped out at the factory
To Mr. Ink and Mr. Pen
And Mr. Thread
And Mr. Money
And Mr. Moon
And Mr. Sun and Mrs. Sun
And to Mrs. Mooney and my mother
And to Mr. Grass and Mr. Trees
And to Mr. Typewriter and Mrs. Typewriter
And to all the others who made
life possible while you were
away in India
eating the natives.

Tom Veitch

NEIGHBORS

Will they have children? Will they have more children?
Exactly what is their position on dogs? Large or small?
Chained or running free? Is the wife smarter than the man?
Is she older? Will this cause problems down the line?
Will he be promoted? If not, will this cause marital stress?
Does his family approve of her, and vice versa? How do
they handle the whole inlaw situation? Is it causing some
discord already? If she goes back to work, can he fix
his own dinner? Is his endless working about the yard
and puttering with rain gutters really just a pretext
for avoiding the problems inside the house? Do they still
have sex? Do they satisfy one another? Would he like to
have more, would she? Can they talk about their problems?
In their most private fantasies, how would each of them
change their lives? And what do they think of us, as neighbors,
as people? They are certainly cordial to us, painfully
polite when we chance-encounter one another at the roadside
mailboxes—but then, like opposite magnets, we lunge backward,
back into our own deep root systems, darkness and lust
strangling any living thing to quench our thirst and nourish
our helplessly solitary lives. And we love our neighborhood
for giving us this precious opportunity, and we love our dogs,
our children, our husbands and wives. It's just all so damned
difficult!

James Tate

THE ORIGIN OF BASEBALL

Someone had been walking in and out
Of the world without coming
To much decision about anything.
The sun seemed too hot most of the time.
There weren't enough birds around
And the hills had a silly look
When he got on top of one.
The girls in heaven, however, thought
Nothing of asking to see his watch
Like you would want someone to tell
A joke—"Time," they'd say, "what's
That mean—time?", laughing with the edges
Of their white mouths, like a flutter of paper
In a madhouse. And he'd stumble over
General Sherman or Elizabeth B.
Browning, muttering, "Can't you keep
Your big wings out of the aisle?" But down
Again, there'd be millions of people without
Enough to eat and men with guns just
Standing there shooting each other.

So he wanted to throw something
And he picked up a baseball.

Kenneth Patchen

BASEBALL

One day when I was studying with Stan
Musial, he pointed out that one end of
the bat was fatter than the other. "This
end is more important than the other,"
he said. After twenty years I learned to
hold that bat by the handle. Recently,
when Willie Mays returned from Europe,
he brought me a German bat of modern
make. It can hit any kind of ball. Pressure
on the shaft at the end near the handle
frees the weight so that it can be retracted
or extended in any direction. A pitcher
came with the bat. The pitcher offers not
one but several possibilities. That is, one
may choose the kind of pitch one wants.
There is no ball.

Tom Clark

PERMANENTLY

One day the Nouns were clustered in the street.
An Adjective walked by, with her dark beauty.
The Nouns were struck, moved, changed.
The next day a Verb drove up, and created the Sentence.

Each Sentence says one thing—for example, "Although it
    was a dark rainy day when the Adjective walked by, I
    shall remember the pure and sweet expression on her face
    until the day I perish from the green, effective earth."
Or, "Will you please close the window, Andrew?"
Or, for example, "Thank you, the pink pot of flowers on
    the window sill has changed color recently to a light yellow,
    due to the heat from the boiler factory which exists nearby."

In the springtime the Sentences and the Nouns lay silently
    on the grass.
A lonely Conjunction here and there would call, "And! But!"
But the Adjective did not emerge.

As the adjective is lost in the sentence,
So I am lost in your eyes, ears, nose, and throat—
You have enchanted me with a single kiss
Which can never be undone
Until the destruction of language.

Kenneth Koch

A REUNION

Week after week glided away in the St. Clare mansion . . .
HARRIET BEECHER STOWE

You will like their upstairs
papered with wrappers off Blue Goose oranges.
You will like their grandmother.
They keep up her grave.
You may get to like them.

James Schuyler

HOLIDAY ON AN ANTFARM

They danced like programmed angels.

In Nature's
most exclusive capitol
they danced
with domestic forethought.

I refuse to say anything dirty about them,
for mud is a fashion
not chosen by the wild ones.

James Tate

Y..r D..k

It w.s c....h f.r t..m to go b..k to t.e h...e
T..y h.d r..d a...t it

I am s.....g d..n to w...e y.u
A...t t..s a.d a...t b....e he d..d
He l...s on h.s o.n f....r a.d s.n

It t..k f..r of t..m to c...y in t.e s......s
F..m t.e s...l s..t g...n p..d
T.e c....g w.s t......e

T.e i.e c..e w..n he w.s w.....g f.r it
It c.....s i....f n..r me
C....g b..k t.....h t.e g....d
D....y c........s
B...k p..e of w.....g
S...e t...e is n.....g b.......l in t.e w.y

T.o w...n f...r w.s c......g t.e w...e
t..t d..t t..t m....r
N.t to c..e b..k w.....d a.d s...n in a s...y

V......e a...e in t.h d........g
O..e u........d we d.......d
T....h it g...s no p......e as d..s w.....r

On t.e s....l b......n b...d
L....s a..........g in t.e h...s
T.e t...g we i........d as a b....e
Or t.o f....s of r.d in t.e t...s
(He w.s w.....g to it)

C.n be k..t in p.....s a.d n.t d.......d k..p
G...g o.f a.y m....t
K..p t..m o.f

To k..p in m..d on a p...h d...g t.e r..n?
No m..e t..n o.....g o...s y....r h..d to l...h
No m..e o.......e to it t..n to a b...n d.g

Ron Padgett

FALLING IN LOVE IN SPAIN OR MEXICO

A handsome young man and a veiled woman enter. They stroll slowly across the stage, stopping from time to time, so that their entrance coincides with the first spoken word and their exit the last.

JOSÉ: I am happy to meet you. My name is José Gomez Carrillo. What is your name? This is my wife. I like your daughter very much. I think your sister is beautiful. Are you familiar with the U.S.? Have you been to New York? Your city is very interesting. I think so. I don't think so. Here is a picture of my wife. Your daughter is very beautiful. She sings very well. You dance very well. Do you speak English? Do you like American movies? Do you read books in English? Do you like to swim? To drive a car? To play tennis? Golf? Dance? Do you like American music? May I invite you to dance? I like to play tennis. Will you drive? Do you live here? What is your address? Your phone number? I am here for four days. Two weeks. One month only. Would you like a cigarette? A glass of wine? Anything? Help yourself. To your health! With best regards. Many happy returns! Congratulations! With best wishes! Merry Christmas! My sincere sympathy. Good luck! When can I see you again? I think you are beautiful. I like you very much. Do you like me? May I see you tomorrow? May I see you this evening? Here is a present for you. I love you. Will you marry me?

GIRL: *(She lifts and throws back her veil, revealing her face,*
        which is extremely and extraordinarily beautiful.)
        Yes!

THE END

Ron Padgett

TO ENGLAND

There are no postage stamps that send letters
back to England three centuries ago,
no postage stamps that make letters
travel back until the grave hasn't been dug yet,
and John Donne stands looking out the window,
it is just beginning to rain this April morning,
and the birds are falling into the trees
like chess pieces into an unplayed game,
and John Donne sees the postman coming up the street,
the postman walks very carefully because his cane
is made of glass.

Richard Brautigan

HAIR ON TELEVISION

On the soap opera the doctor
explains to the young woman with cancer
that each day is beautiful.

Hair lifts from their heads
like clouds, like something to eat.

It is the hair of the married couple
getting in touch with their feelings for the first time
on the talk show;

the hair of young people on the beach
drinking Cokes and falling in love.

And the man who took the laxative and waters his garden
next day with the hose wears the hair

so dark and wavy even his grandchildren are amazed,
and the woman who never dreamed minipads
could be so convenient wears it.

For the hair is changing people's lives.
It is growing like wheat above the faces

of game-show contestants opening the doors
of new convertibles, of prominent businessmen opening
their hearts to Christ, and it is growing

straight back from the foreheads of vitamin experts,
detergent and dog-food experts helping
    ordinary housewives discover

how to be healthier, get clothes cleaner, and serve
dogs meals they love in the hair.

And over and over on television the housewives,
and the news teams bringing all the news faster
and faster, and the new breed of cops winning the fight
against crime, are smiling, pleased to be at their best,

proud to be among the literally millions of Americans
    everywhere
who have tried the hair, compared the hair,
    and will never go back
to life before the active, the caring, the successful,
    the incredible hair.

                                        Wesley McNair

MILK

Milk used to come in tall glass, heavy and uncrystalline as frozen melted snow. It rose direct and thick as horse-chestnut tree trunks that do not spread out upon the ground even a little: a shaft of white drink narrowing at the cream and rounded off in a thick-lipped grin. Empty and unrinsed, a diluted milk ghost entrapped and dulled light and vision.

Then things got a little worse: squared, high-shouldered and rounded off in the wrong places, a milk replica of a hand-made Danish wooden milk bat. But that was only the beginning. Things got worse than that.

Milk came in waxed paper that swelled and spilled and oozed flat pieces of milk. It had a little lid that didn't close properly or resisted when pulled so that when it did give way milk jumped out.

Things are getting better now. Milk is bigger—half-a-gallon, at least—in thin milky plastic with a handle, a jug founded on an oblong. Pick it up and the milk moves, rising enthusiastically in the neck as it shifts its center of weight. Heavy as a breast, but lighter, shaping itself without much changing shape: like bringing home the milk in a bandanna, a neckerchief or a scarf, strong as canvas water wings whose strength was only felt dragged under water.

On the highway this morning at the go-round, about where you leave New Hampshire, there had been an accident. Milk was sloshed on the gray-blue-black so much like a sheet of early winter ice you drove over it slowly, no matter what the temperature of the weather that eddied in through the shat-

terproof glass gills. There were milk-skins all around, the
way dessert plates look after everyone has left the table in
the Concord grape season. Only bigger, unpigmented though
pretty opaque, not squashed but no less empty.

Trembling, milk is coming into its own.

James Schuyler

POTATO

Mysterious murky
Face of Earth

He speaks
With midnight fingers
The language of eternal noon

He sprouts
With unexpected dawns
In his larder of memories

All because
In his heart
The sun sleeps

Vasko Popa
(Translated from the Serbo-Croatian
by Anne Pennington)

OH MY GOD, I'LL NEVER GET HOME

A piece of a man had broken off in a road. He picked it up and put it in his pocket.

As he stooped to pick up another piece he came apart at the waist.

His bottom half was still standing. He walked over on his elbows and grabbed the seat of his pants and said, legs go home.

But as they were going along his head fell off. His head yelled, legs stop.

And then one of his knees came apart. But meanwhile his heart had dropped out of his trunk.

As his head screamed, legs turn around, his tongue fell out.

Oh my God, he thought, I'll never get home.

Russell Edson

DREAM

My dream with its black top
With its white divider with its curves ahead
My dream with its roll of a ribbon with auras of yellow bird
    with its crosses
My dream between cities
My dream with its wild blue air

Ruth Krauss

MATURITY

When you sit at home in a chair
And think about God in heaven
You are probably thinking about something else
It's one of the unfortunate things
That can happen to you in the modern world

That is to say
The time reverts to dusk
And I slack my pace recalling
In my dumb way what Katy Schneeman said
Yesterday which was "Hello" I think
And I'm still shocked when the Seasons
Change
          we've seen that before
My eyes say
The same thing happens!

Dick Gallup

WILLOW PTARMIGAN

Winter plumage
More like snow than snow . . .

   under the northern skies
The willow ptarmigan
Is almost invisible
In the cold breath
Of the eastern Aleutians.
Feathers fallen
From cumulus and snow;
                Two
of the natures of water.

In the wide pulse
Of the north Pacific—
There is water over polished marble
In the green rooms of the sea.
Across our ocean planet
Bad dreams becloud
God's watery parish.
But the eyes of the ptarmigan
Will see me anew.
Truly he loves the part of him
That is within me—
And his white radiance will reveal
A path for me on the charts
            of the winter sea.

John Dimoff

THE MINIMAL

I study the lives on a leaf: the little
Sleepers, numb nudgers in cold dimensions,
Beetles in caves, newts, stone-deaf fishes,
Lice tethered to long limp subterranean weeds,
Squirmers in bogs,
And bacterial creepers
Wriggling through wounds
Like elvers in ponds,
Their wan mouths kissing the warm sutures,
Cleaning and caressing,
Creeping and healing.

Theodore Roethke

DUSK IN THE COUNTRY

The riddle silently sees its image. It spins evening
among the motionless reeds.
There is a frailty no one notices
there, in the web of grass.

Silent cattle stare with green eyes.
They mosey in evening calm down to the water.
And the lake holds its immense spoon
up to all the mouths.

Harry Edmund Martinson
(Translated from the Swedish by Robert Bly)

THIRTEEN WAYS
OF LOOKING AT A BLACKBIRD

I

Among the twenty snowy mountains,
The only moving thing
Was the eye of the blackbird.

II

It was of three minds,
Like a tree
In which there are three blackbirds.

III

The blackbird whirled in the autumn winds.
It was a small part of the pantomime.

IV

A man and a woman
Are one.
A man and a woman and a blackbird
Are one.

V

I do not know which to prefer,
The beauty of inflections
Or the beauty of innuendoes,
The blackbird whistling
Or just after.

VI

Icicles filled the long window
With barbaric glass.
The shadow of the blackbird
Crossed it, to and fro.
The mood
Traced in the shadow
An indecipherable cause.

VII

O thin men of Haddam,
Why do you imagine golden birds?
Do you not see how the blackbird
Walks around the feet
Of the women about you?

VIII

I know noble accents
and lucid, inescapable rhythms;
But I know, too,
That the blackbird is involved
In what I know.

IX

When the blackbird flew out of sight,
It marked the edge
Of one of many circles.

X

At the sight of blackbirds
Flying in a green light,
Even the bawds of euphony
Would cry out sharply.

XI

He rode over Connecticut
In a glass coach.
Once, a fear pierced him,
In that he mistook
The shadow of his equipage
For blackbirds.

XII

The river is moving.
The blackbird must be flying.

XIII

It was evening all afternoon.
It was snowing.
And it was going to snow.
The blackbird sat
In the cedar-limbs.

Wallace Stevens

FOR WHAT BINDS US

There are names for what binds us:
strong forces, weak forces.
Look around, you can see them:
the skin that forms in a half-empty cup,
nails rusting into the places they join,
joints dovetailed on their own weight.
The way things stay so solidly
wherever they've been set down—
and gravity, scientists say, is weak.

And see how the flesh grows back
across a wound, with a great vehemence,
more strong
than the simple, untested surface before.
There's a name for it on horses,
when it comes back darker and raised: proud flesh,

as all flesh
is proud of its wounds, wears them
as honors given out after battle,
small triumphs pinned to the chest—

And when two people love each other
see how it is like a
scar between their bodies,
stronger, darker, and proud;
how the black cord makes of them a single fabric
that nothing can tear or mend.

Jane Hirshfield

TO THOSE WHO LOOK OUT OF THE WINDOW

To those who look out of the window at the night
This passing moment, within the bounds of our city:
We are not many, standing in the dark by the window,
With the cool and starlit air brushing the face
And our eyes hungry for the light-givers,
The luminous ones, brightening the reaches of the sky.
Of them our neighbors, the thousands and the thousands,
Under all the rooftrees in the obscure streets and alleys,
Let us not be reminiscent or piteous,
If, in the coils of the serpent sleep long since,
All unresisting they have become earthen.
—But feel the brush of the wind on the face, the bath
Of the light, the torment of beauty deep in the throat;
And strive, in secret, this brotherhood so small,
To climb the stairway out of the dust a moment
Before the lying down to sleep and the surrender.

Hyam Plutzik

BREATHING SPACE JULY

The man who lies on his back under huge trees
   is also up in them.
He branches out into thousands of tiny branches.
He sways back and forth,
he sits in a catapult chair that hurtles forward in slow
   motion.

The man who stands down at the dock screws up his eyes
   against the water.
Ocean docks get older faster than men.
They have silver gray posts and boulders in their gut.
The dazzling light drives straight in.

The man who spends the whole day in an open boat
moving over the luminous bays
will fall asleep at last inside the shade of his blue lamp
as the islands crawl like huge moths over the globe.

Tomas Transtromer
(Translated from the Swedish by Robert Bly)

FOR YOU

For you, my fellow humans,
Everything is for you,
Nights are for you; days are for you;
Daylight is for you, moonlight is for you;
Leaves in the moonlight;
Wonder and wisdom in the leaves,
Myriad greens in daylight,
Yellow is for you, and pink.
The feel of the skin on the palm,
Its warmth,
Its softness,
The comfort of lying down;
For you are all the greetings
And the masts winnowing in the harbor;
Names of the days,
Names of the months,
Fresh paint on rowboats is for you,
Mailman's feet,
Potter's hands,
Sweat on foreheads,
Bullets fired on battlefronts;
Graves are for you and tombstones;
Jails and handcuffs and death sentences
Are for you.
Everything is for you.

Orhan Veli Kanik
(Translated from the Turkish by Talat Sait Halman)

BUFFALO BILL 'S

Buffalo Bill 's
defunct
    who used to
    ride a watersmooth-silver
                stallion
and break onetwothreefourfive pigeonsjustlikethat
                                  Jesus

he was a handsome man
                  and what i want to know is
how do you like your blueeyed boy
Mister Death

E. E. Cummings

OCEANS

I have a feeling that my boat
has struck, down there in the depths,
against a great thing.
                And nothing
happens! Nothing . . . Silence . . . Waves . . .

—Nothing happens? Or has everything happened,
and are we standing now, quietly, in the new life?

Juan Ramón Jiménez
(Translated from the Spanish by Robert Bly)

DEATH

Going to sleep, I cross my hands on my chest.
They will place my hands like this.
It will look as though I am flying into myself.

Bill Knott

SO LONG

At least at night, a streetlight
is better than a star.
And better good shoes on a
long walk, than a good friend.

Often in winter with my old
cap I slip away into the gloom
like a happy fish, at home
with all I touch, at the level of love.

No one can surface till far,
far on, and all that we'll have
to love may be what's near
in the cold, even then.

William Stafford

VICTORIA

The world is the most that we can see
at one time: a tulip tree and a man
walking a small dog.
The sky, a crystal dome, rests
on the horizon. Beyond this anything might be
imagined or remembered: a horse-headed nebula,
a woman slipping into the water,
you a reader.

A finger of smoke rises out of the valley.
A large puddle has gathered, and so the birds
land, and wash themselves, and take off. I feel
the need to cry—not a lot,
or for long.
                    *

A small boat rising
and falling—we could not have known how
the channel ferry would struggle in the crosscurrent.
He finally sat down, who stood on the deck
watching for the lights of Victoria.
She began to breathe again,
who wanted to hold her breath against the vomit.
                    *
You must not judge us too harshly.
You must not think we left you nothing
but acid rain and that we had no feelings.

What grew grew twisted, knotty, dwarfed.

We left one place, then another.

                                        John Witte

TO THE HARBORMASTER

I wanted to be sure to reach you;
though my ship was on the way it got caught
in some moorings. I am always tying up
and then deciding to depart. In storms and
at sunset, with the metallic coils of the tide
around my fathomless arms, I am unable
to understand the forms of my vanity
or I am hard alee with my Polish rudder
in my hand and the sun sinking. To
you I offer my hull and the tattered cordage
of my will. The terrible channels where
the wind drives me against the brown lips
of the reeds are not all behind me. Yet
I trust the sanity of my vessel; and
if it sinks, it may well be in answer
to the reasoning of the eternal voices,
the waves which have kept me from reaching you.

Frank O'Hara

NO FINIS

When you cannot go further
It is time to go back and wrest
Out of failure some
Thing shining.

As when a child I sat
On the stoop and spoke
The state licenses, the makes
Of autos going somewhere,—

To others I leave the fleeting
Memory of myself.

David Schubert

ACKNOWLEDGMENTS

The editor gratefully acknowledges permission to reprint the following:

"To Satch" by Samuel Allen. Reprinted by permission of the author.

"My Child" from *Poems* by Yehuda Amichai, translated by Assia Gutman. Copyright © 1968 by Yehuda Amichai. English translation copyright © 1968, 1969 by Assia Gutman. Reprinted by permission of Harper & Row, Publishers, Inc.

"Eighteen" by Maria Banus. From *A Book of Women Poets from Antiquity to Now* by Aliki Barnstone and Willis Barnstone. Copyright © 1980 by Schocken Books Inc.

"Spit 'n Image" by Coleman Barks. Reprinted by permission of the author. Published in *The Juice* by Coleman Barks, published by Harper & Row, Publishers, Inc.

"I Would Like My Love to Die" by Samuel Beckett. Reprinted by permission of Grove Press, Inc., from *Collected Poems in English and French.* Copyright © 1977 by Samuel Beckett.

"The Eye" copyright © 1965 by Michael Benedikt. Reprinted from *The Body* by permission of Wesleyan University Press. This poem first appeared in *Poetry* magazine.

"Resolution" copyright © 1969 by Ted Berrigan. Reprinted by permission of Corinth Books.

"Life, Friends, Is Boring" from *77 Dream Songs* by John Berryman. Copyright © 1959, 1962, 1963, 1964 by John Berryman. Reprinted by permission of Farrar, Straus and Giroux, Inc.

"Chronicle" by Mei-mei Bersenbrugge. Reprinted by permission of the author.

"Three Presidents" copyright © 1966 by Robert Bly; "Turning Away from Lies" copyright © 1967 by Robert Bly. Both from *The Light Around the Body* by Robert Bly. Reprinted by permission of Harper & Row, Publishers, Inc.

"Moving in a Caravan (1)" and "Moving in a Caravan (8)" by Robert Bly. Reprinted by permission of the author.

"To England" by Richard Brautigan excerpted from the book *The Pill Versus the Springhill Mine Disaster* by Richard Brautigan. Copyright © 1968 by Richard Brautigan. Reprinted by permission of Delacorte Press/Seymour Lawrence.

"Taking Heart" by David Bromige is from *The Ends of the Earth* © 1968 by David Bromige and published by Black Sparrow Press. Reprinted by permission.

"Lily Flower" copyright © 1969 by Michael Brownstein; originally pub-

INDEX OF AUTHORS

INDEX OF FIRST LINES

INDEX OF TITLES